To Addison Jayne

Mark

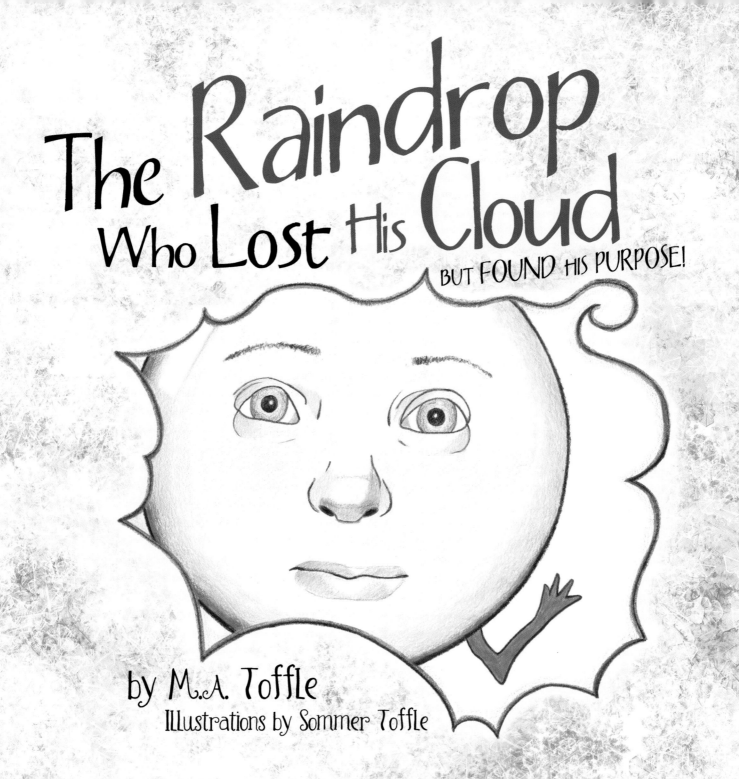

The Raindrop
Who Lost His Cloud
BUT FOUND HIS PURPOSE!

by M.A. Toffle

Illustrations by Sommer Toffle

ISBN 10: 1-59298-353-7
ISBN 13: 978-1-59298-353-7

Library of Congress Catalog Number: 2010935617

Printed in the United States of America

First Printing: 2010

14 13 12 11 10   5 4 3 2 1

Illustrated by Sommer Toffle
Cover and interior design by James Monroe Design, LLC.

Beaver's Pond Press, Inc.
7104 Ohms Lane, Suite 101
Edina, MN 55439–2129
(952) 829-8818
www.BeaversPondPress.com

To order, visit www.BeaversPondBooks.com
or call (800) 901-3480. Reseller discounts available.

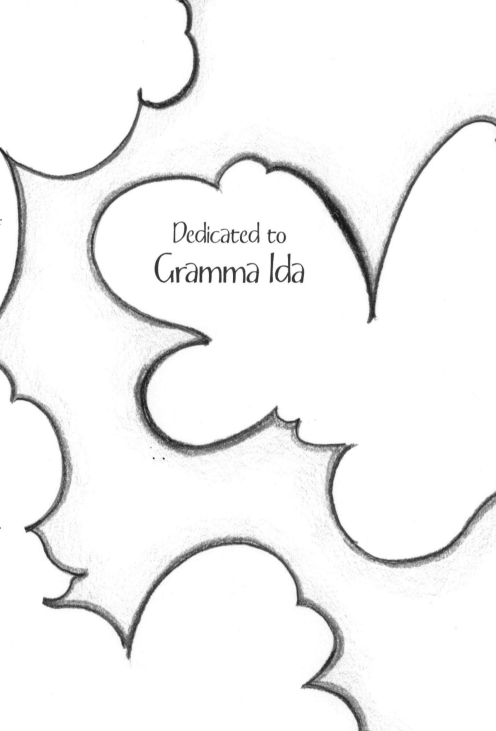

Dedicated to
Gramma Ida

This book belongs to. . .

Addison Jayne

Once upon a time, there was a raindrop named Stewart. Stewart lived in a small, white cloud that floated lazily amidst many others in the late fall skies.

One morning, Stewart awoke wondering, "What is my purpose? All we raindrops do is sit around, sipping on clouds and watching the world go by. I am so bored."

Stewart drifted from raindrop to raindrop in the cloud.
"What is my purpose?" he asked each drop. And he heard the same answer
over and over again: "Why, to grow up and fall to the lands below and go to the rivers
and eventually on to the great ocean."

That didn't satisfy Stewart.

He was afraid he'd fall in the desert and just evaporate away.

Or, even worse, he might fall on a city street and get sucked down into a dark, smelly sewer.

"I want to do more with my life," said Stewart.

"I wonder what the raindrops in other clouds want to do when they get big?"

Stewart's curiosity grew so strong that he went way out to the edge of his cloud
and peered out at the other clouds.
They looked so close, but no matter how loudly he called out,
the other raindrops couldn't hear him.

Stewart felt a strong breeze and jumped on.

Up, up, up he rose toward another cloud.

It looked a bit bigger than his cloud,
and the drops there were bigger too.
They were almost ready to fall.
Stewart jumped off the back
of the breeze and into the cloud.

"What are you going to do when you fall?" Stewart asked his neighbor raindrops. "Why, fall to the lands below and go to the rivers and eventually on to the great ocean," they replied, one after another. "Oh, well," sighed Stewart.

Stewart went back to the edge of the cloud, but now he was all turned around.
The clouds all looked the same! The breeze had shifted too!

He was hopelessly lost.

Stewart cried so hard that he was afraid he would evaporate away.
"Oh, what shall I do?" he wailed.

A big thunderhead loomed downwind of the cloud he was on. "With so much power, maybe the raindrops there can help," Stewart said.

He gathered his courage and leaped back into the wind.

But as he approached, lightning flashed and thunder roared.
Hailstones flew by, saying, "Hop on!
We're gonna dent some cars
and break some windows
before we set off for the great ocean!"

"No, no thanks," replied Stewart.
Off he drifted again.

Stewart felt terribly lonely. Eventually he joined up with a gang of rogue raindrops.
They said that their goal was to just have fun. At last, a different purpose.
"That sounds great!" said Stewart. "Can I join?"
"Sure, come and go as you please! We're easy," they replied.

Stewart and the rogue raindrops spent their time teasing people on the ground.
Whenever a person tried to find the end of a rainbow,
the raindrops would move the end away just as they approached it.

The rogue raindrops danced around the moon in a circle at night.
They made fog banks over roads and rivers to confuse drivers and fishermen.

Stewart wasn't bored, but he felt uneasy about this lifestyle.

There just didn't seem to be **any purpose** to what they were doing.

Eventually Stewart let the wind take him away again.

He drifted higher and higher. It got colder and colder.

Poor Stewart shivered. He didn't have a coat, you know!
He was lonely, cold, and scared.   He was even afraid to cry.

What if he just evaporated away before accomplishing anything?

Just then he heard a small, squeaky voice crying. He looked around.
"Who's there?" Stewart said. The voice said, "Excuse me, but I'm lost."
The voice came from a small speck of dust floating beside him. "Oh, hi," said Stewart.
"Hi!" said the dust speck. "My name is Fleck. I was in the fields down below, helping the crops grow
but it got drier and colder and all of a sudden a whirlwind picked me up. Now I'm up here all alone."
Fleck sniffed. "Will you help me get back?"

Stewart told Fleck how he became lost while searching for his purpose.
"Crops are okay," said Fleck, "but what I'd really like to do is help the wildflowers
at the edges of the fields to grow."
"Say, that sounds perfect!" said Stewart. "Can I do it with you?"
"Of course!" said Fleck. "Flowers can't grow without water."

They talked and talked about it and got more and more excited.

"Can I be your friend?" asked Stewart.

"Oh yes!" squeaked Fleck.

Fleck gave Stewart a hug, and in that instant Stewart felt himself begin to change. He grew and grew and was transformed into a big, gigantic, super-colossal, six-sided snowflake with Fleck in the center.

"Hang on!" said Stewart as the wind caught them.
Stewart and Fleck soared over cities and lakes and fields.
The rogue raindrops had frozen.
They were making sundogs
when they saw
Stewart sailing by.

Stewart introduced the rogue raindrops to Fleck and described their plans. "In the end," he said, "it's not the destination that matters, it's the journey! To help and teach and care for and love others is what makes it all worthwhile."

The rogue raindrops left, and Stewart and Fleck flew on.

They grew more and more exhausted until finally, at dark, the wind calmed and they settled down in a forest glen that would soon be full of spring flowers.

They were so tired that they fell sound asleep.
But throughout the night Stewart's words had been spread far and wide
by the rogue raindrops.

When the sun rose, Stewart and Fleck found themselves surrounded by thousands,
then millions, then billions of other unique snowflakes.
Like Stewart and Fleck, they wanted to do more than just go to the ocean.

In the silence of the forest they could hear a slight hiss
as still more snowflakes joined them.

Stewart and Fleck were no longer alone.
With the arrival of the warm spring sunshine, they would set out together
with their new friends to achieve their purpose.

The End